Groundwood Books / House of Anansi Press
groundwoodbooks.com

We gratefully acknowledge for their financial support of our
publishing program the Canada Council for the Arts, the Ontario
Arts Council and the Government of Canada.

Canada Council   Conseil des Arts
for the Arts   du Canada

ONTARIO ARTS COUNCIL
CONSEIL DES ARTS DE L'ONTARIO
an Ontario government agency
un organisme du gouvernement de l'Ontario

With the participation of the Government of Canada
Avec la participation du gouvernement du Canada | Canadä

Library and Archives Canada Cataloguing in Publication
Sylvester, Kevin, author, illustrator
Gargantua (Jr!) : defender of Earth / Kevin Sylvester.
Issued in print and electronic formats.
ISBN 978-1-77306-182-5 (hardcover).—ISBN 978-1-77306-183-2 (PDF)
I. Title.
PS8637.Y42G37 2019   jC813'.6   C2018-904187-0
C2018-904188-9

The illustrations were done in pencil, pen and ink on bristol board,
with finishing and color added in Photoshop using a Cintiq tablet.
Design by Michael Solomon

Printed and bound in Malaysia

MIX
Paper from
responsible sources
FSC® C012700

In memory of Sheila Barry

GARGANTUA (JR.!)

DEFENDER OF EARTH

KEVIN SYLVESTER

Groundwood Books
House of Anansi Press
Toronto Berkeley

I want to grow up to be just like my mom.

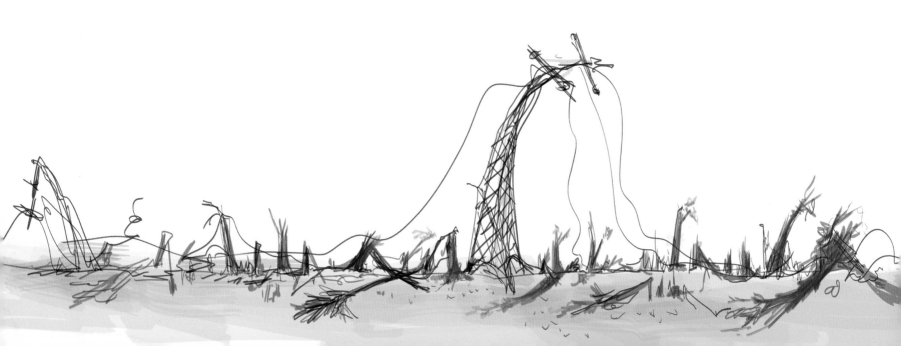

Of course, Mom used to be a little ... wild.

But then I came along.
Now Mom helps fix cities. Even the ones
she used to knock down!

Now she protects Earth from rampaging space robots.

I keep telling Mom I can help, but she says I'm too little. She'll only let me "arm wrestle" our new friend, Zortzon.

Sometimes Mom gets to knock
down old buildings.
I just know I could help!
But she'll only let me watch.

When giant asteroids fly toward Earth, she blasts them from the sky.

She only lets me practice with rocks.
Lots and lots of rocks.

It's time to show Mom
I'm big enough to help.
And I've got a super idea.

And that's just what we do.

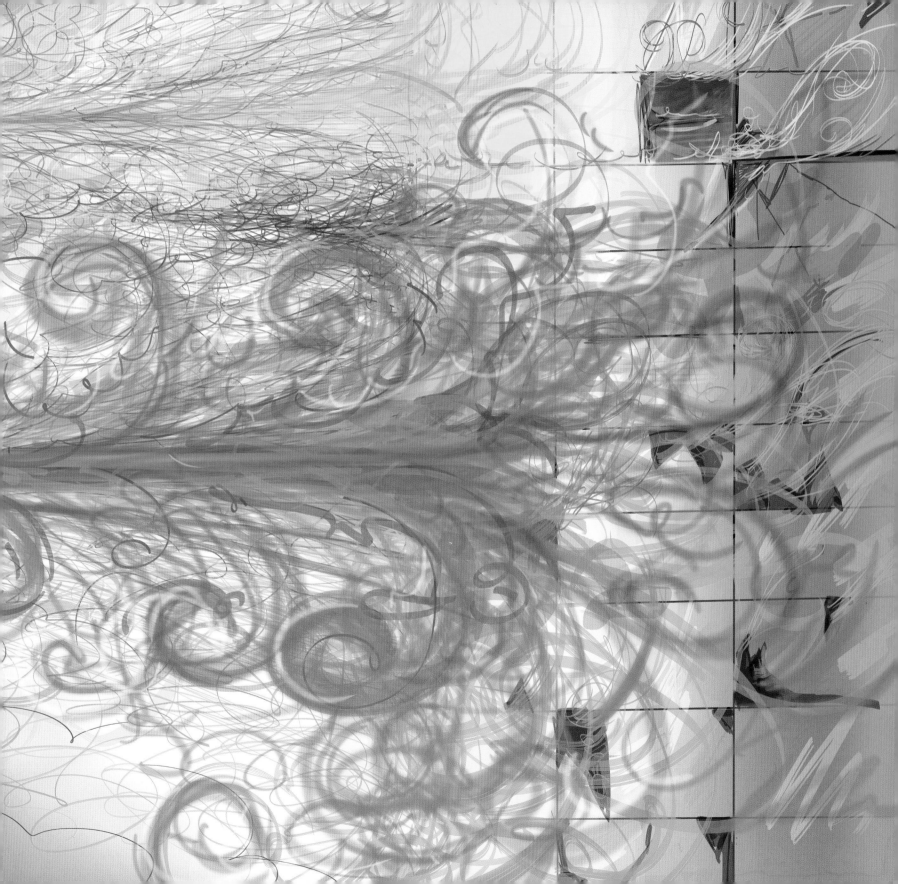

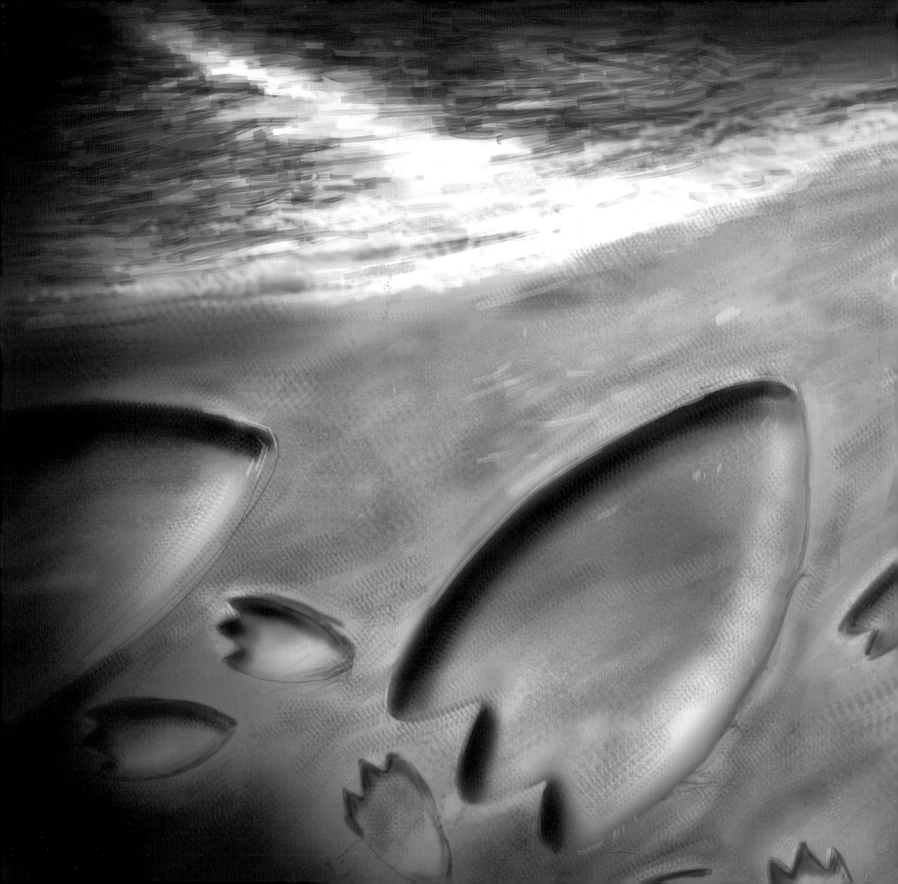